YARDS

CARMEN CAMBRIDGE

CARMEN CAMBRIDGE

YARDS

CARMEN CAMBRIDGE

YARDS

Text copyright © 2015 Jaime Munt

Published by Jaime Munt

ISBN-13: 978-0692597996
ISBN-10: 0692597999

Printed in the United States of America

YARDS

CARMEN CAMBRIDGE

To Mom

CARMEN CAMBRIDGE

CONTENTS

. . .

CARMEN CAMBRIDGE

.

YARDS

CARMEN CAMBRIDGE

CARMEN CAMBRIDGE

YARDS

There is a danger in both belief and unbelief.

~ Phaedrus

CARMEN CAMBRIDGE

What would you do to save your child?

Most parents, when asked this quickly answer, "Anything", without stopping to think what that entails. Our love for our child versus a love for our self and safety. If your child fell over the rail at Gator Gardens, into the muddy brown depth already rolling with large carnivorous reptiles—would you jump in or stand there staring helplessly at an unimaginable horror about to contradict everything we believe about the order of life. Could anyone blame you for being too afraid to do "anything"?

Right now, I lay wondering what before I never doubted.

Am I a good mother?

What if the inevitable, the unstoppable, the undisputable happens—something no mortal being can prevent? How much guilt do we feel when we can do nothing? Do we still feel we should have?

As long as we try, regardless of the impossibilities, then we may live or die feeling like we did the right thing. Right?

So I push myself off the ground, struggling for more than footing—breath, focus, courage—as I find the great dark beast loping out of sight, somewhere in its arms my bleating child and know, I am about to find out.

12 hours earlier...

I hold the weight of my ten month old son on my hip and point at the picture of a man, who I think very handsome. I'm repeating "daddy", "that's your daddy", to the child who will meet him for the first time in three days.

I don't know if I do this for him or me. Probably me, but I think if the boy *knows* him that my husband, Landon, might feel better about being away these thirteen months.

When I say the "d" word, the somewhat chubby infant smiles broadly, the gummy opening shaped like a lemon. He makes a sound of pleasure and bucks a little.

It's hard to feign joy when you miss someone the way I miss his father, but Levi doesn't seem to sense my sadness, merely drinking the excitement in my voice and the frenzy of kisses to the side of his warm, soft head. He feels comfort in the pounding of my heart, just parallel to his own, as the outward voice echoes what my heart has been living off of all week, "He's coming home. He's coming home."

In another room, the microwave beeps loudly and our baby starts wriggling and looking around, greed written across his espresso brown eyes. When I say, "Okay", he knows we're on our way and the squirming becomes almost too hard to control. I can hardly believe how strong he is. Sometimes when I watch what his father can do, lifting things, throwing things, taking lids off jars, I'm astounded by his strength and am glad it's always been on my side.

Our son, Levi, and I have been eating a lot of the same foods since he started cutting teeth. With a grand total of eight, he's got only two less than his great-grandmother.

For supper we're having omelets and macaroni and cheese. I make both in the microwave and, as far as Levi is concerned, something good is about to happen every time the darn thing beeps. I warmed some water for tea a few mornings ago and he kept going back to the kitchen doorway to look for what I made. It went on for hours.

"Num," he says before I open the appliance's glossy black door.

"Nummy, num," I say back. I think he understands this to mean, "*Very* good."

I hear the veranda creak, just as I pull the microwave door open. It sounds strangely heavy, I think, the way the wood groaned.

I know exactly what board is responsible, since I think the sound comes from the east side of the house. More than once that board spared me from cardiac arrest when I'd went out to take in the night air and thought my husband and his friends were deeply vested in talking, sports, snacking, or gaming. Maybe all of the above. But his friend Simon always has and, unfortunately, probably will always like startling me—I scream, wail, shriek, fly through the air and tremble for some time before I can collect my nerves. For Simon, this is great fun and I feel, in some ways, I have to be tolerant because the little shit has been best friends with Landon since they were eight and have gone through hell and back in service together.

It makes Simon happy.

I laugh it off, once I can.

My husband stays neutral.

Other than the flailing child in my arms, all is utterly still, so I decide it must have been nothing and get ready to eat.

Levi slides like a pro into his highchair, no more fighting with frog legs or stiff ninja kicks.

After I dish up our plates, I sit beside him and watch him pinch gumball sized pieces of egg or single noodles, close his fist around them, to ensure they safely reach his already gaping mouth, spread his fingers wide, believing the food therein is still in the center of that hand, and guide it into the eager orifice with his forceful palm.

I watch him for some time, idly picking at my own meal, when I remember something.

So much have I been consumed with my husband's return that I forgot to check the mail yesterday and today. I only remember at that moment, because a significant amount of drool is gathering on Levi's t-shirt and I was supposed to be getting a free sample of fabric softener, after having qualified to do an online survey. I get points for every survey I do. Then, after accumulating so many points, I can turn them in for gift cards.

Shortly before Levi was born, Landon and I felt the best thing to do was give up my job, if only for now, so I didn't have to worry about finding day care. Financially this was doable, but I'd always had my own money. I didn't feel comfortable, for example, buying my husband presents or treating him to special meals with money *he'd* earned. I might as well just tell him what I think he should have and ask him to go buy it.

Sorry. Nope. I can't operate that way. So, while it isn't much, it's 100% mine, however most of what I earn is from babysitting for one of our neighbors Tuesdays and Wednesdays while they have late classes, and from selling handmade cards online.

"Alright stinky butt," I say when he's finished eating and only finger-painting in little smudges of cheese left on his tray. "Time to take a little walk and then a little nap. What d'ya say?"

He gazed around the room, lethargic with fullness and contentedness.

Even though it wasn't cold out, it wasn't warm out either and our driveway wasn't long, but it wasn't the length of just a couple vehicles bumper to bumper either, like the home we had near base. It was roughly one-hundred-and-fifty feet, too far, I thought, to go without putting Levi in something warmer. His little gray "ARMY" hoodie was only just starting to fit him right and was already covered in stains, being I almost always put him in it when we went out or thought it was a little cold inside.

I was thinking about the sound on the veranda when I pulled open the heavy inside door. I wished I wasn't.

The first thing I noticed when stepping out onto our porch was the peculiar odor of beast, but somehow also of man. The strong lingering stink reminded me of the average guy after a hard day's work, should he have spent it laying among filthy mongrel dogs, sour and reeking of musk and open wounds.

Strange… Maybe I *had* smelled this smell before.

I sniffed the air and immediately thought I knew it, but perhaps never so strong. That meant whatever was responsible was close by and for whatever reason the realization of this made my blood run cold.

Our old tin mailbox, little of it retaining its original coat of white paint, seemed a very long ways away. All at once I felt I was five years old and staring across the bedroom at the bunk bed I shared with my younger sister. My right arm raised over my head, hand hovering over the light switch and feeling that I could somehow cross the room and climb the bed before the room was dark and the monsters could reach me.

My heels rocked on the creaking boards as I swayed between a mad dash to the box or one back inside. I hadn't had any reason to run for years and years and thought how foolish I would look if one of our neighbors happened to pass by at that time. They'd tell the other folks in the area, "Boy poor missus Whitfield was charging around her yard, arms pumping, sweating, hair flying, and making time like a tractor in a mudhole."

That was enough to convince me that I was certainly old enough to get the mail by no other means than walking—

even though the thought of taking the truck or four-wheeler crossed my mind.

When I reached the river rock path from the steps to the driveway, my scalp prickled and the sense of being watched was so strong I felt that if I turned around my face would plow into someone or something's chest.

Levi, though with only pale brows to mark it, was frowning deeply and looking around like he noticed something was strange too. I know that babies get a lot of cues from what we are doing and or even feeling, so there was no way to know if he was just picking up on mommy being a little weirded out, the same way a baby animal gets cues on how it should respond from its parent.

Regardless, I took his behavior as confirmation that there was something different outside that day or that moment. Whatever it was frightened me, the integral part of one's being that alerts them to something more than they are— something that can hurt you—whether they have ever known it or not, that warns you of trouble.

Should someone be able to ask the first human being what their gut told them when first they heard a rattlesnake rattle, they would surely answer, "Danger."

Nature offers people a lot of obvious warnings—a lot of them involve teeth or fangs, size, bright colors—but in this case it was stink. Dense, pungent, bestial stink that gave me pause before commonsense stepped in and sabotaged the being it was supposed to advise.

The driveway stretched out before me, more like a hundred yards than a hundred feet. I kept looking over my shoulder, my intuition playing "Red-light Green-light" with something invisible, as yet, to me.

Once I reached the mailbox, had I turned I might have seen when the large dark shape breached the face of the woods at the far edge of our broad back yard. From this far away I would not see its body heaving from its long and urgent dash toward the smell of my sudden exit from my den. I certainly could not see its eyes, the color and brilliance of new pennies, find and fix on me so immediately, one would think it expected me to be there… at last.

As I lowered a little to make sure I hadn't missed anything inside the box, had I looked up right then I would have seen it'd crossed half the back yard.

I squeezed the slight bulge in one of the envelopes, the fabric softener, and told our baby that mommy got a present.

I reached the middle of the driveway. It was coming up around the side of the house. It had been close before, but never as close as it dared come today. No matter how clean, bleached, or rinsed, its keen nose tempted it to our clothesline. When Landon was home, fearfully from the nearest edge of woods it sniffed and snuffed the air of our drying underthings, our sheets. But the man had been away for several seasons and his smell was faint at best.

Then the laundry went up every four days or so, as weather permitted and, every so often, among them were the freshly washed garments from those days when the emotional longing I felt for my unavailable husband left physical traces on the one kind of clothes I had no intention of donning the first day, or maybe even week, after his return.

It snuffed the air and huffed at my fear and the tell-tale yearning for my husband that, for the time being, lay dormant in my consciousness, but only there.

The male babe in my arms smelled of my absent mate and was a threat to anything it sought from me and had to be dealt with immediately.

It took up one of the melon-sized rocks that lined the path to the back yard.

Only twenty-five feet separated me from the house.

Levi seemed particularly still, like a tiny kitten that'd clawed its way up your shirt and is afraid of falling.

The smell of animal was stronger. Faintly did I even taste it in my mouth. I felt the rush of a half-dozen large spiders up my back and settle on my neck and scalp. So when a horn blared twice on the road behind me, I screamed loudly, squeezed the baby too hard, and my knees almost gave out.

Startled too, the creature ran away, with such speed that in mere seconds the only trace of the forest which devoured it was the wavering of the trees and underbrush, like ripples on a dark wall of otherwise still water.

I waved at the older man and woman in the big red GMC. It was Cletus and Jenny Lee Farther. They were backing up and pulled into the driveway. The wife's hand hadn't stopped waving from before her husband even laid on the horn—even though he told her, "Her back's to ya, she cain't see yit."

"Sorry for frightnin' ya," Cletus apologized, "but we just wanted to say 'hi' and check on you and the boy."

The boy, was bawling now.

"We're alright," I told them.

"A little jumpy? A little chamomile tea and a touch of honey would soothe a tornado," said the woman in the passenger seat.

"You know, actually, I don't know if you can smell that, but I think some animal came around the house today. My husband says bear stink like pig sty. Is that true?"

"So far as I know it," said Mr. Farther.

I thought so. The news didn't comfort me any more than if the smell *had* been that of pigs, because I didn't want bear coming close to the house. But because it didn't smell like pig, or not completely, I could only wonder what was responsible.

I asked the couple if they could smell it. They wrinkled their noses at the air and Jenny Lee said, "I sure smell *something*."

"That's the smell alright. Ever' so often I catch a whiff of that stink—you never forget it—" I thought I'd smelled it before too, I injected "—but hell if I know what it is. Jasper Scott and I were cleaning a deer out by his barn one time and it came on powerful strong. The animals in the wild got flighty and them in the barn were spooked like a cat in a dog kennel."

"What do you think it is?" I asked.

"Well," he made the "l" sound last at least five seconds, "folks will always have their theories, but if you ask me it doesn't matter what it is, because whatever it is spooks just like any other sane wild thing. They don't want nothing to do with us. A pig might go missing. A fence might get broke, but the worst people ever get is scared. That goes for bear, wolves, lions, what have you, I'm sure."

"You old fool, like you know a damn thing about lions!" Cletus's wife scolded.

"Well," the same long "l", "if people live in straw huts, no guns, no hounds, not much for clothes, and had been doing just fine for hundreds or thousands of years before us folks started givin' 'em those things, then I think I'm right to think somethin' stops the lions from eatin' all of 'em."

"For Pete's sake," was all Jenny Lee could say.

"Mark my words," he said to me seriously, "am'nimals will always be more scared of you than us. I mean more scared of us than we are them."

That sounded right, but was hard to remember. Would be really hard to remember facing down a bear, wolf, or lion.

"Your hubby got guns?" Mrs. Farther asked.

A small laugh followed the smile that bloomed on my face, "This *is* Georgia and my husband's a serviceman who enjoys hunting."

I do too.

"Just so you got 'em should you need 'em," Cletus said.

Landon once told me, unless I thought I could pull the trigger on someone that I was better off forgetting we even had guns. We hunt for meat not sport. Would I pull the trigger on some animal that was stinking up my yard and scaring the Dickens out of me? You bet.

"Weeeell, we gonna git on. You need anything you give us a holler."

I told them I would and we went inside.

The creature had just returned to the fringe of the back yard, its heart pounding in terror and anger.

I was back in the den, it felt, even though its senses could not yet tell it yet with certainty, its gut did not require any proof to think I was inside. It knew anyway.

The baby was crying. The sound made it want to howl with rage. It was being taken care of. Attention. Affection. The smell of my favorite perfume filled its memory the way a word comes forward in your mind when you think of what you want to eat, want to watch on TV, or who you love. Should any other woman wear it, until faced with her, she would be me it thought, it sought, it found. But the likeliness that any of the few other ladies in a fifteen mile radius wore Miss Dior was unlikely. Had it not been our five year anniversary, it might have been unlikely for me too, since I like a lot of other perfumes that don't cost a lot.

Woe to that poor woman who should wear this perfume within smelling distance of that creature, because one of the worst things a thing can feel is their hopes dashed. They would be, when the smell did not match the woman it was supposed to belong to.

Then it would get mad.

Woe to any living or inanimate thing in the wake of its anger.

We planned on getting a dog after my husband retired from service. The plan had changed from retiring at forty to retiring at thirty-four, when Levi would be starting Kindergarten, because Landon didn't want to be away so long when our son would be old enough to want him to be there. It was hard enough for my husband to miss anything, but to miss things his child would want him there for was when he thought it could start to hurt our child. Whenever Landon wanted or needed to be done with service, I told him I would stand behind whatever he decided. That I would do my best to make sure that our son knew the difference between absent and neglectful. Between responsibilities and priorities—that if daddy's responsibilities conflicted too much with his priorities (us) that daddy would come home as soon as he could and never go away again. And that was true.

Always did I miss Landon. I don't remember ever thinking, gee I'm glad I have a little time to myself. Never, when he was home, did I feel it was interrupting the routine I made in the life I lived when he was gone. We are some of the lucky ones, as far as making this kind of life work. Most people don't want complicated. Patience is something they demand, but refuse to give—the same with understanding.

For this, the beast hated Landon.

So rarely did it dream, a close semblance to human dreams, but when it did its mind was inundated with murderous fantasies… of tearing my husband apart.

I wished so bad that we had a dog, but until my husband was out of service it wouldn't be like a family dog. It might not think of Landon as part of "the pack". If it was a good guard dog, there was no way this would sit well with any of us.

I didn't know any of our neighbors to be without a dog or two or four.

The beast panting at the woods' edge would have never come close enough to regard our family differently than other people, whom it tried vainly to avoid, had we owned a dog of any kind.

It was well aware of this fact. The absence of a dog was one of the first things that it noticed about our property. The menace. The threat. The *warning* was missing.

Intelligent and curious, some time ago, it decided to take advantage and steal close to our house one balmy summer night, the bedroom window half-open and the sound of heavy breathing softly purged into the night air.

There it stood enrapt.

Only when dawn broke did it think to leave, did it think anything at all beyond what it smelled and heard.

When Landon got out of bed and started talking to me, it ran like hell back to the safety of the dense forest. Even though it felt like it had a brush with death and was petrified at its poor judgement and thought it should never come back, it still did. And it didn't know why, but it didn't feel like its choice anymore.

Shortly thereafter I'd sometimes find my clothes having come off the line and, more than once, had some articles of Landon's clothes go missing altogether.

Mostly it was underwear, but my husband's favorite shirt disappeared. The next day Landon found a few scraps that were left of it and blamed it on a neighbor dog. I told him if he let me wash it more than once a year it wouldn't interest animals so much.

It remembered when, in the most ungodly hours of morning, Landon snuck up, under the reek of its own being, and spackled it with one purposely close, but intentionally non-lethal shot from his 12 gauge Mossberg. My husband said there was a prowler. After that, the thing never came around when it knew Landon was home.

But Landon wasn't home and we didn't have a dog.

I didn't mind using a gun outdoors, but it didn't feel right having one ready inside the house. I didn't even want to think of ever firing a gun in my home, especially with a child. Gunfire isn't something anyone should hear in a home. Everything about it seemed wrong or unsafe without the weapon being in my husband's hands. In that case I felt untouchable and incredibly attracted to him for making me feel so safe.

The next best thing I could think of was a baseball bat. Bear, wolf, lion, or man isn't going to be a fan of taking a one and a half pound aluminum rod to their head at eighty miles per hour.

I made sure all the doors and windows were locked and the curtains were drawn. When we lived on base and in town we had black out curtains, but being out in the middle of nowhere we opted for a lot of opaque shades which didn't seem to offer any privacy now, even though the only thing that got through them was light… and the shape of anything moving on the other side of it.

I found the bat, while bouncing Levi into a better mood, and went to run his bath. He dazedly watched the bubbles grow, still rounded tears laying on his ample cheeks. I brushed them with my thumb and forefinger, privately noting the wetness still in his eyes and making his short dark lashes cluster. I kissed the side of his head, saying how sorry I felt, but falling short for words that equated my actual feelings.

I checked and rechecked the water temperature—I was wondering if I would be so neurotic with our next child, should we have one—and was just about to lower him in when I heard the deep groan of the bad board on the east side of the house.

A tremor coursed through me—inwardly, outwardly—obviously.

I heard my breathing.

Heh... Heh... Heh... as it moved across my teeth, my mouth slightly open as I listened, as if this would help me hear better. Other than what I could not help, I did not move. I did not so much as blink.

Was this to be more silent that I might better hear? Was this to be less noticeable, so that we were safer? All I know is that I felt like moving was a fatal error.

Levi splashed loudly as he struggled against the hands cupped under his armpits. He wanted his toys, the octopus and turtle he loved more than me sometimes. More often have I heard him cry to be separated from them than being separated from me.

I gave him his things and tried not to think about what I heard. It was then that I considered calling the police and asking them to take a look around. I was ready to site the prowler my husband had seen, even though that was a couple years ago.

After some thought I was too embarrassed to bother them with what ultimately added up to a board that needed to be replaced. So I let it go and would forever wonder how different things would have been had I swallowed my pride and made the call someone this scared should make.

Had I been a deer or a squirrel, the police would have been on their way, but humans readily abandon their instincts. There are good reasons and bad reasons for doing that. Some of the good reasons are that people are animals and sometimes animal instinct tells people to do things that are wrong on almost every level, like submitting to sexual or violent impulses. Some instances when it's bad that we ignore our animal instincts is when our gut tells us something, someplace, somebody is wrong.

What was that about being better safe than sorry?

People can be convinced or convince ourselves to forget this too, in fact, we often do.

So while I was telling myself it was nothing and shampooing the silky pile of hair on our son's head, the bipedal anomaly was checking the house for a way in. It understood that glass can break, but it also knew that glass can hurt and it's dense, leathery fingertips were not dexterous enough to pinch out slivers so fine as we humans are able, especially with the availability of tweezers.

It had seen doors open, but didn't fully understand the mechanics.

Once it had come upon a small pill-shaped trailer house, which then served as a hunting shack, and, after returning to it again and again over the spring and summer to no sign of human occupancy, finally got the nerve to investigate. After a short time it found the handle of the screen door. It easily yanked the light metal rectangle wide on its hinges and spring which complained loudly when opened, startling the creature to promptly release it. The door banged shut loudly. A thin trail of urine marked the path of its escape. Ever since, it had been shy of doors.

In the back of its mind always lay the possibility of the man's return, the same way I always hoped Landon might be coming home earlier than he told me to expect him. In complete ignorance I'd left the scent of fear in the air and, with face pressed to the frame of our front door, it drank the inferred tension and excitement the way two people on opposite sides of a room may be drawn to one another in tangible attraction, without so much as one verbal suggestion that when they leave they will leave together, but they know it all the same.

Had I been in the foyer just then I would have been close enough to hear it grunting and panting at the narrow fissure between it and the stronger scent of me. The popping sounds it made with its mouth sounded like the nervous smacking of a bear. The frustrated whine was grossly similar to the helpless bawling of a cub left behind or in a tree. But, had I actually been in the foyer just then it would no longer have huffed and puffed, but thrown itself through the flimsy front door and probably the heavy door too.

When you're that close to something you want, almost to the point of madness, how could you ever let it get away?

Levi was out of the tub and was lost somewhere in the towel gathered around him. He was laughing, especially when I dried his ears. As adults we are conscious of everything, the sound of our voice, the way we chew gum, what direction do our feet point when we walk, conscious of even our laughs. Baby's laugh uncensored. They don't care if they sound dumb or if they are being too loud. The raw joy of their belly laugh might be a fair substitute for antidepressants, unless the absence of such laughter is the reason you are on them. All I know is that the sound of it makes my heart feel huge in my chest and all my secular problems seem distant or vastly unimportant. It is like the ultimate affirmation that I am doing the right thing for our son. This being our first child, I always worry. And I don't want to ruin him—my husband has been away since I was three months pregnant, I am the only one to blame if he isn't healthy and happy.

"Where's Levi?"

A huge helium laugh erupts under one crumpled end of the towel.

When I lift up the end he drops down hard on his bottom and is laughing so hard he seems completely senseless. I don't want him too wound up because I'll be putting him down in about an hour. I don't really want to.

It's not safety that I need in him, that's ridiculous, but it's his company I want so bad that I consider depriving him of some sleep. When our baby is laying down I feel solitude like I have never known before motherhood. My mother-in-law says this is just because I'm a fretful first-time mother. I think I'm just alone too much. I was used to working. Used to seeing friends more regularly than I have since we moved out here. Yes, we live some distance out of town and away from base, but there are a lot of other factors too. Some people don't want to make the effort to stay friends after people move or change jobs. People make new friends, as they should, but have a hard time juggling too many or keeping in touch with people they aren't seeing every day. That incentive is gone.

My parents live in southern Nebraska and Landon's live in Mississippi. Landon has bad feelings about some of our neighbors, though few and far between. Darren, one of Landon's army friends, occasionally checks on me when my husband is deployed, like my husband checks in on Darren's family.

I was too pregnant to feel comfortable driving or trying to shop alone and he'd come over to help. We were a few miles down the road when we passed one of our neighbors checking his mail. I was about to raise my hand and wave when Darren caught it and pushed it down at my side.

"Don't communicate even that much with that guy," he said. I asked why. He said I didn't need to know why, but I better not so much as smile at him and, should the guy ever show up at my place, I needed to lock the doors, grab the Beretta, and take the phone into a room I could lock and call him or the police. No questions asked.

Ever so slightly my eyes widened as I thought over again the warning and what he told me I should do. Call him, he said.

I should.

I diapered the pee machine and took him to the nursery for pajamas. The tot seemed conscious of the huge weight that suddenly lifted off of me. Either genders have strengths and weaknesses and I don't care if it sounds antifeminist when I say that I feel comfortable to leave my husband to take care of things he says he will take care of. Men seem to be so capable, either by virtue of already knowing or of the good sense to reason through a problem. Men take care of stuff. Men make me feel safe, if they don't make me feel creepy.

Ordinary men have the innate ability to make people feel safe. Imagine then, if you don't already know, having your husband or boyfriend, and all the friends of his you trust and like (if even begrudgingly) being mostly servicemen of any kind—police, firemen, marines, whatever—Lordy! That's a lot of comfort.

I was humming when I stepped out into hall. The faintest whisper of air made the fine loose wisps of hair below my ponytail brush against my neck.

I slowly turned, but only a few degrees lent my peripheral a preview of the heavy dark beast towering at the end of the hall.

This, the kind of moment that happens and you're supposed to—in some panic—reel around and realize you'd hung up your long black trench coat in the hall instead of in the closet. You're supposed to see it's just a door open into an unlit room. You're supposed to be able to explain it away. You're not supposed to see a reason to be scared.

So far up my throat did my heart jump that I could not breathe or scream around the lump.

Its massive form was, if not for its neck and shoulders, almost dome shaped. Against the light in the hall, its reddish-brown eyes blazed like polished bronze in its thinly haired face. It looked like an ugly, dark, muscular man with severe hypertrichosis. Its tall and heavy brow sunk deep as it frowned at me. Its wide flat nose flared hugely over its grimacing thinly lipped mouth. The teeth beneath its pale gummed mouth were whitish-yellow like antique whalebone. To me, there was nothing human about them— even if there really was—it might as well have been the maw of a great white shark. It was huge and monstrous, and teaming with dangerous looking teeth.

It knew I was somewhere very close from the moment its great leathery feet lit cautiously upon the first interior floor. It had deftly climbed onto the roof over the veranda, loudly, but not loud enough for me to hear over the water while I rinsed our son. It went to an attic window where it easily pulled out the storm window and went through the screen on the other side.

Through the floor it heard me playing with Levi and, under the baby's unfettered laughter, it creaked across the dusty attic boards until it knew with every ounce of its being that I was right below it. Probably, it thought, could it get through the line of smooth flat trees and snatch me up through the hole it made. It wouldn't matter then if it killed the baby or not because it would die without me. If it still wanted to, it could take its time and finish it later. It thought it would like that, if only to hurt the man or assure that the man would not be able to save it, should he come back in time.

If it could not get through the trees then this would alert me and I would flee. It wasn't going to take that chance.

It had only reached the hall when I began to hum. It listened intently and, for that brief moment, forgot what it was doing. It forgot until the door opened and I suddenly appeared in the hall.

Animals are not without feeling and its emotions and reasoning were certainly complex enough to compare to that of a young human, while its instincts and self were of a matured being. My scream invoked no feelings of shame or sympathy, only the reality that I would try to get away.

The force of the angry cry it made resounded through the house like a black-metal singer roaring through a loudspeaker.

The sound of it charging down the hall might as well have belonged to a bull, if it too were so large and heavy to make the pictures fall and windows rattle.

I flung myself into the nursery. The door was locked the very instant it was reunited with the frame—the slamming sound was like a gun going off in my ear. The baby was suddenly in my arms. Then I was yanking up the window and punching out the exterior screen. I leaned through the window and felt horrible when I purposely dropped the baby to the decking.

I used to know how to do this, get in and out of windows without getting hurt. Head first, feet first, I couldn't remember and it didn't matter because I was already going through and was not about to go back in.

The nursery door flew inward, hanging off the, now bent, lowest of three hinges. I fell awkwardly on my arms and head, then shoulder and side. My only afforded consciousness was that I did not hit the baby and actually had to roll to one side so my legs did not come down on him as I spilled out on the wood.

Levi was crying. Then he was in my arms, the cries abbreviated by being bounced as I ran.

It grabbed the open portion of the partially breeched doorway and tore it free from the last hinge to get in. The sound of running on the deck enraged it. Turn back, leave through the attic, leave through another door, find a way out—another way out, never crossed its mind.

Glass and broken framework clattered across the nursery floor and veranda.

It knew how to crawl or leap out of places without being hurt, all that hurt was the glass which it loathed, but was too mad to even notice. Not even the sound of it shattering registered alarm, as one would expect.

On hands first and then feet it found the familiar air and falling night. It ran quietly on these, without wasting time to stand. It cleared the railing, following not the sound of the infant's cries—to which it was barely conscious—but the untainted essence of fear and female tracked mere seconds through the smell of grass, wood, and earth.

Propelled by the combined effort of four powerful limbs, the beast almost sailed past the small shed where the fragrance suddenly veered.

The door rattled shut.

In a hurry to stop, the creature hunched and curled into a shapeless mass of fur. Many other people saw it plainly with their eyes, but crouched and undiscernible from shrub, shadow, or moss still could not *see* what they had seen. Now, the bulk of hair and muscle unfolded. It erected to a daunting eight feet and some inches to spare, no straighter could it stand and maintain a comparable balance when on two feet.

Its rounded, muscular chest heaved as impatience and adrenaline coursed through it. I saw the thing approaching, its somewhat long arms swaying purposely under broad, but sloping shoulders. This was the gait of someone about to kick someone's ass and me and the baby were the only ones there.

It snorted and snuffed as it came near, but it knew exactly where I was and I knew it knew. The only secret between us, as the shed's doors swung wide, was what I had in my hands.

A similarly deafening roar poured out of its straining mouth, but the pitch was distinctly pained, as well it should be when an ax sinks into you.

I didn't see clearly where the blade found purchase, just that it was somewhere high and to its left side. I was having trouble dislodging it and, as the thing thrashed in pain, had some trouble getting my hands on the handle at all.

While it was hurt I didn't want to let it go or give it a chance to come after us again.

To hell with the ax, I thought. There are lots of para-weapons out here. The only problem was that it was getting dark and it was getting hard to see them. I tried to remember what was where. I knew where the shovels were. The rake. Beside me I knew there was the long handled, pelican beaked branch clipper.

What I snipped didn't matter, just that sometime when I opened and closed the small powerful steel mouth that it cried out in pain.

It heard the metal jaws as they bit and pulled its long, dense hair. It shoved at the thing as it fought out the sharp wedge of metal in its chest and then, felt it bite a finger. Felt and heard the crunch of bone as it clave the digit like a sapling poplar. The surge of new pain temporarily distracted it from that in its chest and shoulder, thinking nothing as it tore the ax free and threw it an unimaginable distance into the nearby woods.

It did not know words, and could not form them anyway, to cry "You bitch!" at me, but the wail driven through the small enclosed space delivered the message loud and clear.

It reeled off somewhere to the west, the left side of the shed, and I took the opportunity to throw open the light metal cabinet and retrieve the bawling and disoriented baby from the level where work gloves, masks, and rags are stored safe from mice.

Several times did its dangerous arms sweep so close that the wretched feel of them brushing me still lingered on my arms and hands. I was sure that if they had struck true that I would be laid out or somehow broken. What would that mean for Levi? Nothing I could live with.

I bolted like a rabbit and made for the back steps, the closest to the nursery window. I am proud that I remembered that I locked everything, even though I might have wondered then how the creature invaded our home. How that happened wasn't a priority and by the time I figured it out I wouldn't care. What I cared about at that moment was the broken glass all over the deck and nursery floor. I didn't know how to get in without taking the chance that Levi would get hurt.

I gave myself an abbreviated second to come up with a solution before running to the furthest corner of the porch and seizing the top of one padded wicker chair. It sounded loudly as I dragged it back to the window. I rotated the chair so one arm was against the siding of the house. Then I plopped Levi on the cushion.

I figured that I should be able to crawl through the window and have him be high enough up that I might reach him inside.

Reaching through the demolished window frame, I tore down the curtain rod, and hastily gathered the thin fabric on the window ledge before climbing through. I was wishing the windows were like that at my in-laws'. Those tall and wide windows could be easily stepped through from ground level, but Landon and I had liked the security of the inside floor being slightly raised and windows slightly higher so that one could not stand flat footed outside the house and look in, not unless he was eight feet tall.

I did not pass through unharmed, but I didn't think any life threatening injuries could come from the glass or splintered wood, so I tried hard not to think about where I was cut. All I was thinking was that I left the baby outside with that thing and that had to be addressed right now.

I leaned through the space and was able to get a decent enough hold on one sleeve to pull Levi enough that he tried to get up. I pulled him inside, without so much as glancing around—pointless waste of precious time. Were this a movie, I would have surely dawdled at the window, looking left and right, making a "sexy" pout while my tousled ponytail fell loose and beautifully around my carefully scuffed face. Only, after some time, when I saw the thing returning, would I try to get the baby in and then, with impossible difficulty.

While the movie me would have still been at the window, we were in the hall. I was wishing Levi was in a harness so I could be hands free. I thought about the nearest gun. It had to be a hand gun unless I found somewhere safe to hide the baby so I might strike out to finish the monster on my own.

I wasn't about to do that.

I only wanted the gun if I could have it in a matter of seconds. I was only going to mess with the creature again if I had to.

It would take almost no time to grab my purse and fly out the kitchen door into the garage where a truck with a full tank waited. Rarely did I see less than four bars on my phone, which was always in my purse which always held my keys. I could grab the gun in the bread box above the fridge as I rush through. Armed, out the door, and on the phone. Sounded like a good plan.

Outside the creature clutched his wounded hand, which concerned it more than the large pink mouth opened on its upper left chest. The more pressure it put on the severed limb the better it felt and the more focused it became.

I would return to my den, which it knew humans to do, most the time, when they are scared. Stupid, it thought, that they should lead things directly back to what should be their refuge, especially when there are young kept there. No animal would do that, they would run the opposite direction, if given the choice. But an animal would never make their den so obvious either. In my stupidity, it thought I deserved whatever happened. None of this swayed its curiosity of me, in fact, it was visibly mounting.

A snarl fixed on its evolutionarily bastardized features. Some aggression from a female, it thought, was normal, as long as the baby still had breath.

I snatched up my purse and moved on to the gun, in haste, completely overlooking the cell phone charging on the counter next to the mail. I threw back the stainless steel lid of the breadbox. It took a second longer than I expected to get down the gun, which was considerably easier for my husband to reach. I unlocked the back door and the truck simultaneously, heard the "chug-chug" sound of the locks unlocking. The headlights and taillights flashed. I yanked open the passenger seat, threw my purse into the driver's seat, and fairly slung poor Levi between the seats and into the child seat in the back of the cab. I clipped this into that, unfocused and less concerned with the small seatbelt than what I'd just fought outside.

I jumped into the passenger seat and climbed behind the wheel. I swore loudly when I realized I'd forgotten to close the passenger door.

I stretched across the seats, the gear shift driving angrily into my side, and clawed the far swung gate. Just then, I looked up at the hairy giant rushing through the kitchen.

I yelped.

Lunging forward, I caught the shallow trough handle in the door where I always stick the napkins from fast food places, much to Landon's annoyance. The door swung shut. A few unused napkins flap in the impact and spill out when I pull my hand away. I hit the lock button. I look up, through steamed glass at the enraged primate glaring through it.

Springing back, like a punching bag, I recoiled against the driver's side door. The thing raised a large bloody fist. My palm slammed urgently against the wheel—blaring the horn again and again. I looked away one second to see where the horn was on the wheel, because I never use them, and when I looked back it is gone or, at least, out of sight.

Behind a Velcro closure on the outside of my hunter green denim purse is the pocket with the truck keys. I fumble with them and, of course, they fall to the floor, but within seconds they are in my hand, along with several grains of sand under my nails.

The garage door opens steadily—I'd every intention to waste no time with it, but feel I can spare a second to not do massive damage to our home. How would I explain that? How can I explain this? Everything I know about lore, mythology, cryptozoology, urban legends, amounts to very little, but one doesn't have to know much to know when they are seeing something so obviously not anything else.

No bear. No person in ape costume. No hallucination. No misunderstanding. No hoax. I knew exactly what I was seeing from the very first I saw it, even though I paid very little attention to the myth—if I could think of it as such anymore.

Who was going to believe me?

Why is this happening, I thought as I hastily drove the key into the ignition. I thought they were supposed to be peaceful. Shy. Gentle giants, at least compared to their Himalayan cousins.

BAM!

The truck's end swung wide to the left. Under the pounding sound of my heartbeat in my ears, I hear Levi coo happily at the motion. The engine turned over easily. I look over my shoulder just as the creature charges the tail again, with enough force this time to force the rear bumper all the way to the wall, where it collided loudly. Several tools clattered to the ground.

The beast roared savagely at the thing encapsulating us.

I looked over my shoulder. Our eyes met. Diabolical madness red in its smoldering stare. I threw the truck into drive. It threw itself one last time against the side of the truck, howling loudly, painfully, with effort, swinging the truck wide. I'd slammed on the gas, but rather than the driveway, I was staring down the interior wall of the garage.

I shoved the gear stick forward, the black "R" turning orange as it shifted into position. I pressed too hard on the gas, but it didn't make any difference for or against me, the tail was already against the wall. And then it went through it.

"No!" I cried and threw myself between the seats to pull the baby out of his. My instinct was to run, realizing the truck blocked its path outside, but I didn't count on that stopping it for more than seconds, because it hadn't had much trouble moving the pickup already, to say nothing of scaling it. If it started to break in, Levi would be on my lap and out the door I would go, but for the moment this was some safety, though there was no way to determine how much. False security, a voice in the back of my head was saying. Probably there was no other place as safe, though.

I scrambled for the phone, turning over my purse in the seat. It took me several seconds to realize what you already know and clearly did the image of it laying there rise up through the dark recesses of memory, like the message in a Magic 8 ball, except mine read:

"You moron, it's in the charger!"

With very little difference in the size or broadness of a fox trap were the open jaws of the thing roaring at me through the glass. I laid on the horn again, this time without letting up. It stopped screaming and stared at me with the stillness and decisiveness of an assassin. My body went cold and I started shaking. Levi was crying again. I might have been crying, but was too scared to be entirely in myself anymore. In some ways I was going numb. Maybe I was going into shock.

It examined me through the glass. Did not understand why I kept fighting. Did not understand why I'd bother. Nature is so. We are of nature. It's the strong who survive. It was infinitely stronger than the virtually hairless female pressed into the corner of the vehicle.

Submit, its eyes were saying.

Desperation read in the wet eyes staring back and yet she still did not accept her place.

It slammed its fists down on either side of the window, thinking "Come out! COME-OUT-*NOW*!!" and bringing its fists down heavily and frustrated.

I turned off the truck and took back the keys. Levi, in my lap, was looking between it and me in fretful anticipation. I reached for the handle and cracked open the door. Immediately, the thing started to hoist itself up, making the truck complain and rock as it added the weight. I pulled it closed and locked it again. It slid back down.

"What the hell do you want?" I murmured. At the sound of my voice its face changed, to signify no emotion as I knew it. I have always thought, when you smile at your dog, what message are you conveying? The expression the beast made meant nothing to me, but because it meant something to it I found it terrifying.

I moved Levi between me and the door, put the key back in the ignition, and turned on the battery. The baby strained to try and see my right hand, because it just heard something click.

The female's expression changed, it looked peaceful.

My jaw set and I slowly lowered the passenger side window, while simultaneously raising my right hand. At the earliest moment the towering beast started to shove its hand through. I did not expect or appreciate the strength of it or its earlier efforts. The passenger side window exploded as it strained through with one hand, pulling with the other. A thousand cubes of glass speckled us, the seat, floor, and the beast. At the sight of glass it recoiled, but flung itself back at the truck just in time to see the handgun level at its face.

It had seen guns before.

BLAM!

It reeled back, crying out. I took a second shot when its shoulder passed by the window.

Shoving the door open, baby clasped to my hip, I ran around the front of the vehicle, but it was too far and wide for me to get a shot at the floored monster. I cursed, which I am usually careful to not do in front of Levi. I felt bad and wished I hadn't, but mama needed to get a good shot—hell, any shot, but I wasn't going back through the truck and I wasn't going to put the baby down so I could climb over it.

I thought maybe if I stepped on the tire I could get enough height and leverage to put a few more rounds in the groaning ape, but that was when I heard a vehicle approaching and all I cared about was getting away.

I spun on my heel and ran.

I wished I had taken the keys out of the truck, as the house keys were on the set, to say nothing of leaving the battery on. You can't make mistakes when it's life or death.

Though it had not yet hurt or technically attacked us, I was pretty sure that its intentions weren't good.

I saw headlights skimming across trees as it worked around the two sets of curves to the left, or west, of our property. I watched the pine trees, ink black in the darkness of night, turn a smoky green-blue as they drank the brief caress of light. Then both headlights appeared, I was a third of the way down the driveway. I waved my free arm as it was about the pass, standing about twenty feet from the road. From my point of view, I swear I saw a thread of light lay across the very edge of us as I ran toward them. I think they had to have seen me. I screamed after them.

Maybe it was the gun in my hand.

I didn't want to go back to the house, but if there was any life in that thing and it thought to come after us again I did not want to be on its turf. I could not outrun it. I couldn't lose it in the woods, even if I was stupid enough to go running off into them in the middle of the night. The nearest neighbor was a little walk away, but too far to go in the dark, even if I didn't have to worry about that creature.

I wished there was a safe place to leave Levi so I could deal with this on my own. Probably I should have put Levi in the truck, climbed on to the roof and emptied the gun into it. But there was glass on the seat and, if it were able, could easily reach in, reach the baby.

So what should I have done?

What can I do?

I stared at the dark garage, trying to pierce the darkness and see if it were standing right there, or if it were laying where I left it, no longer moaning, but still and dead.

I giggled, feeling a little hysterical. I was thinking about what would happen tomorrow. What would happen when I called the police and they saw what I had shot down in my garage. Brag to my husband—boy wouldn't he be surprised when he came home!

Guess what I did when you were gone, Landon?

I imagined turning the body in for a reward, paying off the house, fixing the garage. I snickered loudly. Levi laughed that I was laughing.

Suddenly we were doing exactly what I didn't want to be doing, heading exactly where I didn't want to be heading. I thought of the phone. The guns. Places we could hide. I was thinking of the four-wheeler, electric lights, places where I thought we could survive until the police came. I imagined telling Darren to bring guns—lots of guns!

I was grinning foolishly and shaking like a leaf when I climbed the steps to the front door.

Locked.

I knew that, of course.

Where's your head? Where's your head? Spinning. It was spinning its tires. And I was quaking, a seven point five, so hard that I was visibly jerking. Making our way through the dark, I knew I was close to the truck when the sound of my shoes announced we were now on concrete. I followed the truck—oh my God what had I done to the truck—to the garage!? I shook so hard I almost dropped the baby. My fingers felt like ice. I choked on the stink of the beast. Still there. It was still there, but where? Too dark. Too dark. I yanked open the truck door and reclaimed the keys.

I frowned, salvaging a portion of my sanity.

Why is it *so* dark?

I looked around the room, in my mind's eye, trying to remember if I remembered right, but I thought that the kitchen door was open.

The light was left on. Yes, I clearly remember, because I saw that thing coming at me while the passenger door was still hanging open. Come to think of it, there should have been quite a few lights left on, I think.

I was suddenly wary of the house, like it had betrayed me. I didn't know what it meant, but this was not a change in my favor. I didn't believe that the thing cut the power, but I did believe that it wouldn't have any use for light the way that humans depend on it. The damn thing navigates just fine in dense wilderness, swamps, rugged terrain. It was a horrible blend of the strengths of animal and man. So it was smart.

Smart enough to know that the only one benefitting from lights was me.

I didn't want to go inside. It was in there. It must be in there. The stink, the horrible reeking odor was everywhere—so much so that there was no way to distinguish where it was stronger or weaker—it just was. As constant and unwavering as the darkness. There would be no forewarning. Silently would it traverse the house, much as it had when it first breeched the security I thought we had by locking doors.

If I couldn't go inside, then where could we go?

What do I do? I whined to the only person that could help me. Me.

I just needed one damn phone.

The flimsy outer door sounded loudly, like someone pulling a bow long and unskillfully across violin strings. At the main door, the key sounded loud as it slipped into the slot. The knob seemed to creak, the door groaned loudly as I pushed it open. Cringing at every sound I made, straining for any I didn't, I went into my own home, my sanctuary, feeling utterly terrified. No one should ever be afraid in their home.

I listened hard, heard nothing. I sniffed the stinking air, it meant nothing. To my right, about six feet away, was the counter where I lay the mail. I didn't want to fumble in the dark. The dark was its friend, not mine.

I threw the switch for the kitchen. Nothing happened. I switched it back. Nothing. There are four switches by the door, the kitchen, the porch light, the "foyer" light, and a switch for the yard light.

I turned on the yard light. The large amber colored dome on the electric post cast a strange colored illumination on the greater portion of the yard, but made all the shadows without just that much deeper.

So, not until I turned on the porch light could I have made sense of the great looming shadow immediately behind me on the porch.

Even then, I didn't see it and it was well aware that most the time, unless a human lays its eyes on you (and sometimes not even then) will it be aware of you.

It had been seen many times and not *seen,* but I wasn't even looking.

I turned on the light in the entry and, to my great relief, found myself alone—at least as far as I could tell.

When the entry light came on I was able to tell where my cell phone was, without guessing. The other phone in the kitchen was by the doorway to the garage and I sure as hell wasn't going over there.

Levi was excited about something—fussing, whining. I moved my fingers under his bottom and could tell that he'd dropped a load at some point, but could not tell that this was not the reason for his whimpering. Reason being, I'd never heard him whimper like this before.

It looked down on me, bleeding, hurting, but all of that forgotten in feeling vindicated for all of it by the triumph it felt now. Were it not in so much pain, it would have made small puffing sounds, grunting sounds, that were natural to its being, but it'd stiffened against the pain and only now, its delight superseding its suffering, did it snort and snuff quietly, but not so much so that I did not hear it.

It smelled as much as sensed my fear peak—sensed me spooked. It grabbed me by one arm and my pony tail and yanked me backward off my feet. Levi landed on the ground partially underneath me and I, underneath its strafing legs.

The baby was crying.

It shook my head. My neck screamed. The world rocked as it dropped me and I tried to lift my head. It grabbed at one of Levi's exposed legs. The baby screamed. I reeled on the large leathering hand and bit the mouth of the severed finger. I felt its hot blood course newly across my mouth as I leaned back from the wounded hand and the inevitable thrashing that seemed to follow every injury it suffered.

It grabbed the back of my jeans, trying, I thought, to get me on my knees. It grabbed hold of my hair again. It tried to make sense of my clothes, wringing his hand into the back of my t-shirt. Shaking the belt loops until they broke.

I hit the ground hard, with my right elbow, trying to distance Levi from my thrashed body and to also keep the gun in my hand.

Suddenly the thing pulled up on my hips. I felt the futile driving of an appendage against me. Heard the grunts change. The whines change. The whines became more whiney, higher, frustrated. The grunts became lower, longer.

It roared and thumped harder against my jeans, an utterly foreign barrier that, like skin, as far as it could tell, was not something that could be taken off or ripped away.

When the belt loops tore, it thought it hurt me even as it smelled no blood.

The clothes it often inspected as they were drying on the line merely carried a scent and had nothing to do with a human's strange appearance. This was not the way I looked when it spied on Landon and I that first night.

How to find the female it'd seen that fateful night was beyond its comprehension until the back of my shirt slid up.

"What's this!?!" its body language might have said, were it a human, as it held up the back of my shirt and looked inside.

It dropped me again.

I took the opportunity to roll on my side, then I would blow it away once and for all.

Though it wasn't beyond me what the thing was trying to do, I had only subconsciously registered its nakedness before then. Above its knees were large rounded thighs and a long muscly stomach that I might have expected to more resemble that of a gorilla, for some reason, but it was far closer to human than ape, had the muscles not been defined to a degree beyond human limitations without the intervention of drugs. The part of it I was staring at, be it apelike or otherwise was beyond me—who would know— but it looked very human to me, if only grotesquely large.

I raised the gun. It smacked my hand. The gun flew. My hand folded to one side, my pinky lay flat against my arm. I heard the snap. Felt the pain, which was too big, apparently, to come out of my mouth.

It looked across the woman, doubling over in pain. The strange weapon lay at a harmless distance. What more could I do to it, it wondered. My nails, like any other humans, are thin and flimsy, by comparison to its own. In my case, they were short too and carefully rounded so I might never accidently scratch the baby or draw blood on my husband's back. Human teeth are short and weak. Our jaws small and strengthless. Our bodies small and helpless, without the aid of tools. Different than a female of its own kind, the thing admired the smallness of my being and the largeness of my breasts and hips.

It breathed the fragrance of my perfume mingling with the essence of missing my mate and took in the nearest sight of me it'd known.

The female looked up at it fearfully, painfully, with eyes that struck it as somewhat large now that it could see her well. Despite or because she was different than the females of its own kind, its need grew only stronger.

It was ready to try again.

If it had been a man, I may or may not have been able to reason with him, but I didn't even have the luxury of trying. If this were a movie I would have started cooing to it, stroking its legs, hoping that the big dumb beast would think I decided to be compliant and then do as much damage as I could, when I could.

I was about as helpless as I could imagine being. If I hurt it now, without killing it, the thing need only stomp its foot once and crush my skull or Levi's. It need only smack me across the face—it broke my wrist and could break my neck as easily. It might be able to grab my skull and squeeze until it collapsed inside its palm. Even if I didn't fight, there was no guarantee it would not kill me after. I didn't even want to imagine the damage that thing would do.

In our house, if it's worth having, it's worth fighting for. I just couldn't figure out how.

Lowering on its haunches like a sumo wrestler, the hairy stinking creature tossed me like a pancake. I landed slightly on the baby again, his bawling was like a storm siren against my ears—should I have been sitting beside the speaker.

It found the top of my jeans and discovered where they were not fused to skin. It pulled on them, but succeeded only in lifting me up. It made a fist around the top and shook it. When I hit the floor this time, I thought to do something I never thought I'd ever do to anyone.

I turned over on my side and kicked up between the legs straddling me. The testicles were raised, but never as far as my heel drove them, when I crushed them and the lowest portion of its phallus.

Its cry was a close semblance to that when the ax struck true. I'd hurt it bad. It folded in on itself while I scrambled to get out of its reach. Despite its pain, the last thing it wanted was for me to get away, and managed to catch the back of my pant leg.

I kicked back with my other foot, making contact with the rough end of the denuded finger bone.

I cheered inside at the intensity of its wail.

Baby snatched up on my hip. The phone came off its cord. I ran through the kitchen, crunching across a shattered bulb. The truck blocked the exit through the large garage door, but the backdoor was close. The creature was getting close too. Even as I yanked the backdoor closed behind me did I hear the booming sound of its pursuit. In the kitchen. I would be in the garage. At the garage door.

I heard it howl in rage exactly when I thought it should— having turned the lock on my way out. After half a pause it slammed through the door, tearing it clear off the frame.

If I could get far enough ahead now, I knew I would be okay. I was going somewhere it wouldn't get us. In its wildest dreams it couldn't.

Foolishly, perhaps, did I allow the confident smile of success as we whipped around the corner of the house, heading for the road. The yard light on the electric post illuminated the exact area where we needed to go.

Injured, the thing gained on me.

Against the starless dark surrounding our dream home we emerged into the strange yellow light of the yard. In the distance, too far to savor more than a cloudy hue of light, but near enough that it would overcome us before even we were truly illuminated, a monstrosity, existing to many only in folk lore, closed in on a mother and child.

I knew I could fit in the culvert, having once hid there when Landon dared me to find somewhere I could hide that he couldn't track me. It wasn't comfortable, but I could get in, which meant Levi would easily fit and probably be able to sit up, but that skunk ape was out of luck. I could take my time, make all the phone calls I wanted.

It lost.

Oof!

I hit the ground hard. The world spun on a wheel of blinding pain. My teeth felt bent, my jaw fused. A single tone, like old TV station signoffs, rang in my ears.

Wetness tickled the side of my face as it ran over my skin— sweat I thought, because the tickle of sweat is familiar to almost anyone, therefore the obvious culprit, but it was blood.

Consciousness came and went, the stink of the beast constant, its cries intermittently far and near, angry and sometimes in considerable pain.

Several times my body was knocked roughly and once I was stepped on by something incredibly heavy and incredibly wide.

When at last my vision cleared enough to tell something my mind could understand, it was the strange grayness of dawn that makes light, shadows, and the gray in between muddled like paint in water.

Clearly though, did I see the thing standing over me, even though I'd no strength to look higher than its knees. It bowed to prod my shoulder and the side of my head. I tried not to blink, that it thought I was dead and was glad it thought that.

For the longest time, as we lay in the yard, I didn't hear Levi crying. I didn't know what it meant. If it meant anything, I didn't want to know.

What could I do?

I didn't know that there was even more of me than this head—not even neck or shoulders for it to sit on. I'd no other feeling than the pain which was everything. All else was a phantom consciousness of Levi—of his existence—which, dead or alive must be, though I could not touch, smell, feel, or hear him, he had to be, by virtue alone of my love for him.

After what seemed like an eternity, the thing must have been satisfied that I was whatever it wanted me to be—it did nothing to turn the tables for or against my being dead, if that is what it hoped. When it no longer felt it had to shove on me, it leaned past me and, when it straightened, the sound of our baby's crying arched over me.

To my surprise and its, "No!" groaned loudly through my clenched teeth. It was a "no" with finality. The "no" that broke the camel's back. The "no" that makes one shut up and listen. The "no" that says I'd rather die than say "yes".

But at the sound, it fled.

The sound that erupted from my unhinged jaw was like the scream of a braking train. I tried to get up, but couldn't. I clawed at the grass, but could not find myself in it. Was I paralyzed, broken, spent to nothingness after this night of hell?

It was heading for the woods.

I pushed against the earth, dirt ground under and into my nails, my chin, and brow as I tried to use them as leverage, the same way Levi did when he was first learning how to get up.

What if I couldn't get up?

What if I'd nothing left?

And what if I was too afraid to follow it into *its* home?

Am I a good mother? Do I have to be to do what I need to do? Am I a bad mother if I can't?

The sound of Levi's bawls were fainter.

If someone asked me what I would do for my child, I'd answer, "Anything."

Let's find out.

Where I lay and where I stood were, for a few seconds, indistinguishable.

Had someone happened by at that moment, and clearly saw the person standing unsteadily in the yard, very well they might have greeted the day thinking they'd seen a zombie. Would they have shot me? Before the 21st century I would have thought "no". These days…

I managed a step. It didn't feel reliable. Pain shot through my limbs. It's just pain. I tried another. *Oh my God, oh my God, oh my God! I can't do this!* I forced the next. I took the step after that. I heard the dull thumping of my shoes as I crossed the dewy grass. I heard the loud puffing sound of my breath. Then the thumping was louder and closer together and didn't think of each step—I shouldn't. I couldn't. I allowed anger to exchange despair as the fuel of my gait. I started to feel less.

The most important thing was closing the distance, but in the back of my mind I knew that reaching it meant finishing this. I needed a weapon and became vaguely conscious of the ground as I followed the path its large heavy frame carved through the wild grass growing on the northeast face of the property.

What if you don't find one?

"I'll use my bare hands," I muttered.

The woods were dark as night and I was hesitant to enter, only until I heard Levi crying from much closer than I thought possible with how swiftly it moved. Perhaps I would find it dead, having finally succumb to one wound or another. Maybe it had found a trap, though I couldn't imagine what would happen if something with feet of its size stepped on a small animal trap, even one with teeth, or even a bear trap—its feet being so wide. I imagined its foot being folded like a body in Stephen King's *Mangler*.

I seriously doubted stepping on a trap would stop or slow it.

Following the sounds of his cries as best as I could, I was vaguely aware that his was still being moved, but very slowly. So little sense of self had I, in such pain, that I'd no idea if the thing succeeded in what it tried before. Had it not, I thought, and it planned to use Levi as leverage, then I just might be able to save him. I don't know how much time I lost, but I know I lost some. If it hadn't, I didn't know what would have stopped it.

Light, though weak, began to reclaim the wilderness from night, and it was then that I saw the shape of it beyond a dense stand of trees. Our eyes met.

I wanted to say, "Give me back my baby" or "Stop" or "Put him down", but I said nothing. I don't even know if I could.

More urgently now did I scour for a weapon, but could attain nothing, but a branch and even that, only if I was able to break one off, because the forest floor was still a blanket of darkness.

Were there one I could break off, this would not speak well of its integrity to break that thing.

What did it mean that the thing stopped fleeing? I wondered as I closed in on it.

I circled enough that I put myself between it and the direction it looked like it meant to go.

Levi's light gray hoodie looked bright against the shadows and the dark beast clutching him to it. Its massive hands spread out across the infant's struggling body. Against the light fabric I saw two large and complete hands. By comparison, though reeking, this thing was clean. No blood. No wounds. Had I been able to see, instead of sense it, I would have known its penny bright eyes were full of fear.

I tried to say, "Give me back my baby," by the sound that came out was little more than static.

I looked at Levi.

It looked at the baby and back at me.

When it lowered its long powerful arms merely inches, more like a gesture of the baby toward the ground, it hesitated and looked at me, watching, with eyes that had little trouble with the dark, as a fleeting expression of relief passed through my strange, almost hairless face.

It let its arms down more, the look of relief transformed into a look of hope until it backed away.

I took a step forward and it took three back.

So I took my foot back and the baby came closer to the ground.

Like an elevator dependent on moving backward for the car to come down, did it lower Levi to the earth. Once grounded, the creature skittered back as far from the infant as I of them.

I did something stupid then, I ran to my baby. Had it meant to distract me, I'd have fallen for it. Had it meant to bait me... I was doomed. It could reach me in seconds, kill me easily, while I was preoccupied with the Levi. But it didn't.

I looked at it as I knelt to reclaim my crying child.

It watched me, almost softly, though its body was clearly stiff with fear. Its body...

I saw through its long fine hair the more sparsely covered swells of small breasts. My eyes widened.

Was this the difference between the demeanor of these things, I wondered as I stared at this impossible second creature.

I glanced down at Levi and, but for the rustling of the underbrush, she had vanished.

What had she meant taking the baby? Was it because she thought I was dead? Where was the male? Why didn't she hurt us?

Not until we returned to the yard did I know.

The beast's massive form lay out like a gingerbread man near the edge of the lawn, his head caved in by a large, club-like branch lying beside him. Tufts of fur lay scattered. Some of the clumps were still attached to portions of skin with deep red undersides.

It would destroy me, I think, if Landon was ever unfaithful to me. Even at a zenith of rage, I would never conceive of or commit murder, especially for an error of that nature, but some people *have*.

Most that think murder don't submit.

Humans readily abandon their instincts.

Animals… or those not far removed, do not betray their instincts or let anything betray them.

CARMEN CAMBRIDGE

YARDS

The story you've just read was inspired by events that took place over one night, in southern Arkansas, in the early 1970's.

The actual individuals subject to the unidentified being's torment were several teenage girls.

CARMEN CAMBRIDGE

YARDS